# A is for....

## After-dinner chocolate

Roald Dahl and his family ended
each meal by delving into Roald's
red plastic box – a gloriumptious
treasure trove of chocolate treats
– and picking their favourite.

## Allsorts, Liquorice

One of the delicious treats that was often
hidden away in Roald Dahl's tuck box when
he was at school. Another favourite was
liquorice bootlaces. However, young Roald
tied himself in knots when he was told the
stringy sweets were made from dried rats'
blood! You can read all about it in **Boy**.

## Aztecs

An ancient Central American civilization who *really* loved their chocolate! It is said that Aztec Emperor Montezuma drank fifty golden goblets of bitter chocolate every day!

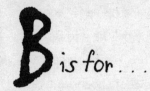

# B is for...

### Beards

Why use a fridge, when a beard is the perfect place to save chocolate, dried-up scrambled eggs, spinach and minced chicken livers until later? Just ask Mr Twit.

### Belgium

Would you believe that a country as small as Belgium is the third biggest maker of chocolate in the whole world?

# Roald Dahl's Incredible Chocolate Box

Illustrated by
## QUENTIN BLAKE

Hungry for more delicious
facts about Roald Dahl?
Visit the official website at
**www.roalddahl.com**

PUFFIN BOOKS

Published by the Penguin Group
Penguin Books Ltd, 80 Strand, London WC2R 0RL, England
Penguin Group (USA) Inc., 375 Hudson Street, New York, New York 10014, USA
Penguin Group (Canada), 10 Alcorn Avenue, Toronto, Ontario, Canada M4V 3B2 (a division of Pearson Penguin Canada Inc.)
Penguin Ireland, 25 St Stephen's Green, Dublin 2, Ireland (a division of Penguin Books Ltd)
Penguin Group (Australia), 250 Camberwell Road, Camberwell, Victoria 3124, Australia (a division of Pearson
Australia Group Pty Ltd)
Penguin Books India Pvt Ltd, 11 Community Centre, Panchsheel Park, New Delhi – 110 017, India
Penguin Group (NZ), cnr Airborne and Rosedale Roads, Albany, Auckland 1310, New Zealand (a division of
Pearson New Zealand Ltd)
Penguin Books (South Africa) (Pty) Ltd, 24 Sturdee Avenue, Rosebank, Johannesburg 2196, South Africa

Penguin Books Ltd, Registered Offices: 80 Strand, London WC2R 0RL, England

www.penguin.com

First published 2005
1

Text copyright © Roald Dahl Nominee Ltd, 2005
Illustrations copyright © Quentin Blake, 2005
All rights reserved

The moral right of the author and illustrator has been asserted

Filmset in Gill Sans and QuentinBlake
Made and printed in England by Clays Ltd, St Ives plc

British Library Cataloguing in Publication Data
A CIP catalogue record for this book is available from the British Library

ISBN 0-141-31959-3

## Bogtrotter, Bruce

He's a champion among chocolate chompers!
When Matilda's horrid headmistress, Miss
Trunchbull, forces him to eat a huge, gooey
chocolate cake, he bravely obliges in one go
... Burp!

## Butterscotch and caramel

Vile Crocky-Wock-the-crocodile thinks this
sweet topping spread on little girls makes
a super marvellous lunch treat. When
crunching little boys, mustard is much
preferred. It makes your eyes water just to
think about it!

# C is for...

## Cacao beans

The magic ingredient in chocolate. The beans grow on cacao trees and amazingly, out of 10,000 blossoms, only twenty to thirty become the pods which hold the beans. This makes chocolate a most precious thing indeed!

## Cadbury

Roald Dahl and his schoolfriends thought themselves the luckiest boys in the world. They used to give marks out of ten for never-before-tasted chocolate bars sent by Cadbury, whose chocolate factory was near to their school.

# Charlie and the Chocolate Factory

After he'd finished writing this book, Roald Dahl asked his nephew Nicholas what he thought of it. 'Rotten and boring,' replied Nicholas. Roald rewrote the whole book and now it's a classic. Forty years after it was published, it still sells a mind-boggling phizz-wizard amount of copies every year.

# Charlie's chocolate prison

In an early version of **Charlie and the Chocolate Factory**, Charlie tumbled into a chocolate mould that was used to make life-sized chocolate boys. But by the time the book was published, this part of the story had disappeared – presumed melted.

## Chocoholic

A person who absolutely,
totally, utterly loves chocolate.
Roald Dahl was a complete
chocoholic.

## Chocolate milk

A deliciously slurpable treat, usually made with
milk and chocolate powder. But according to
chocolate supremo, Mr Willy Wonka, what's
the very best way of making chocolate milk?
(See answer below.)

## Chocolate-ometer

You can tell how chocolatey a chocolate bar
really is by reading its wrapper. Milk chocolate
contains about twenty-five per cent cocoa solids
– the stuff that makes chocolate taste of
chocolate – while dark chocolate can contain
up to seventy-five per cent cocoa solids. Yummy!

**Answer:** Keeping chocolate cows!

## Chocolate remedies

Doctors once treated coughs and indigestion with chocolate. Much tastier than cod-liver oil!

## Cosmic chocolate

On 29 June 1995, chocolate was a gift exchanged between Russian cosmonauts and American astronauts above the Russian space station Mir. This wasn't the first time chocolate played a part in the space race. Three American astronauts, named Shuckworth, Shanks and Showler, also had a close encounter of the chocolate kind – when a certain Mr Wonka rocketed past in his Great Glass Elevator.

## Crocodile food

According to the Enormous Crocodile, there's something even more tasty than a bar of chocolate ...

'I'm off to find a yummy child for lunch.
Keep listening and you'll hear the bones
go crunch!'

## Curious concoctions

Roald Dahl invented the marvellous and magnificent marmalade and bacon sandwich. Have you ever tasted one?

# D is for . . .

## Doggy treats

Both Roald Dahl and his dog loved Smarties. Chopper the Jack Russell terrier chomped four after lunch and four after supper. He also ate oysters, caviar and, occasionally, dog food.

# E is for . . .

## Easter-egg hunts

Roald Dahl loved Easter – it was his favourite time of year. He thought that

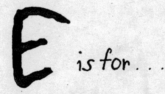

*'Easter is as lovely as Christmas is horrible.'*

He especially loved the eggstraordinarily eggciting and eggstremely eggstravagant egg hunts he went on as a child.

## Energy Balls

In 1936, Forrest Mars, the founder of the famous chocolate company, took a pea-sized piece of dough flavoured with malted milk, exploded it in a vacuum and covered it with melted chocolate. He had invented the Energy Ball! Never heard of it? That's because it was quickly renamed the Malteser.

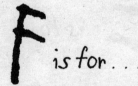

# F is for . . .

## Favourite lunch

Roald Dahl loved prawns so much he ate them for lunch every day. They had to be

Norwegian prawns, which he ate with mayonnaise and lettuce. Followed by a Kit Kat, of course.

## Fickelgruber, Prodnose and Slugworth

These are Willy Wonka's arch-enemies – they'll stop at nothing for his secret chocolate recipes!

## Filling

Check out these crazy creamy fillings invented by the chocolate genius, Mr Willy Wonka . . .

Dairy Cream      Coffee Cream

Whipped Cream

Violet Cream      Pineapple Cream

Vanilla Cream      Hair Cream!

## Fillings

What you get if you don't keep your teeth clean!

## Fruity free-for-all

Roald Dahl had seventy fruit trees in his orchard – apples, pears, plums and cherries. There was too much fruit for Roald to eat, so he invited the children from the local village to help themselves.

# G is for...

## Grand High Witch

The Grand High Witch hid her evil Delayed Action Mouse Maker in a bar of chocolate which she then gave to the greedy little boy, Bruno Jenkins.

## Grubber

A rare name for a sweet shop.
(Peep between the covers of
**The Giraffe and the Pelly and Me**
to find out more . . .)

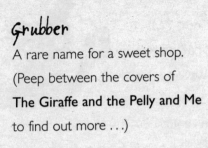

# H is for...

## Hair Toffee

A wig-fuzzler of an invention from the
wonderful Willy Wonka. Eat just one tiny bit
of this toffee and in exactly half an hour you'll
sprout a whole new head of luscious locks.
As well as a moustache and beard worthy
of Mr Twit!

## Hot chocolate

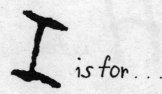

Chocolate was first enjoyed in Europe in the seventeenth century. But it was made into a drink to be sipped from cups, not unwrapped from shiny paper. The first proper chocolate bar was not invented until a hundred years later.

# I is for...

## Invent your own chocolate bar!

Roald Dahl used to dream of inventing a world-famous chocolate bar that would amaze and astound the great Mr Cadbury himself. Why don't you give it a try? Would your chocolate bar be crunchy or squidgy?

Would you suck it slowly or gobble it up in one go? Here are some possible scrumdiddlyumptious ingredients to get you started…

Biscuit          Caramel

Ginger     Chilli     Honeycomb

   Hundreds and thousands

Nougat      Nuts      Lemon peel

   Rhubarb   Raisins

              Oh … and chocolate!

# J is for...

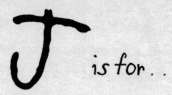

### Jujubes

One of Willy Wonka's strange
but delicious sweet creations.
Mint jujubes will give you green
teeth for a month!

# K is for...

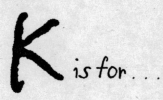

### Krokaan

A crispy kind of toffee made from butter,
sugar and almonds. And one of Roald Dahl's
scrummiest Norwegian treats.

# L is for...

## Loompaland

Where Oompa-Loompas come from. It's a dreadful place, packed with hornswogglers and snozzwangers and those terribly wicked whangdoodles.

# M is for . . .

## Mayan

The Mayan Indians not only discovered cacao
trees growing in the rainforests of Central
America, but used the cacao beans for food
and money. Just like the Oompa-Loompas in
Willy Wonka's chocolate factory!

## Missing chapter

A chapter called 'Spotty Powder' was
originally included in **Charlie and the
Chocolate Factory**. But there were too
many naughty children in the earlier versions
of the book, so 'Spotty Powder' – and the
revolting Miranda Piker – had to be dropped.
Turn to page 45 to discover it for yourself . . .

## Mole

Not the furry animal
with the big paws, but
something much more delicious.
Mole (pronounced mo-lay) is a spicy Mexican
sauce made using both chillis and chocolate. It
is often poured over turkey.

## Mouse surprise

Mrs Pratchett, the owner of
Roald Dahl's local sweet shop,
was a mean old lady. So a
young Roald and his mates
decided to teach her a lesson.
When her back was turned,
Roald popped a cold, stiff,
dead mouse into a jar of
gobstoppers. (You'll find the
whole squeakingly good story
in **Boy**.)

# N is for...

## Naughty children

Never disobey the very wise Mr Willy Wonka or you might end up being flung down a rubbish chute, stretched like a piece of elastic, squeezed up a long thin pipe or even turned into a giant blueberry!

# *O* is for . . .

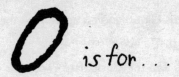

## Ooh la la!

Roald Dahl's favourite French
meals were foie gras
(a very rich liver paté),
mussels and snails (minus
their crunchy shells, of
course!).

## Oompa-Loompa secrets

Writing – like inventing magical chocolate
bars – can be very difficult and brain-aching. It
often needs many attempts to get something
just right. There were four earlier versions of
**Charlie and the Chocolate Factory** before
Roald Dahl felt he'd written a brilliant book.
Take a top-secret peek at an early version of
the Oompa-Loompas' song about greedy

Augustus Gloop and compare it to the longer rhyme that made it into the final version of **Charlie and the Chocolate Factory**.

The Whipple-Scrumpets ... began dancing about and clapping their hands and singing:

'Augustus Gloop! Augustus Gloop!
The great big greedy nincompoop!
How long could we allow this beast
To gorge and guzzle, feed and feast
On everything he wanted to?
Great Scott! It simply wouldn't do!
And so, you see, the time was ripe
To send him shooting up the pipe;
He had to go. It had to be.
And very soon he's going to see
Inside the room to which he's gone
Some funny things are going on.
But don't, dear children, be alarmed.
Augustus Gloop will not be harmed,

Although, of course, we must admit
He will be altered quite a bit.
For instance, all those lumps of fat
Will disappear just like that!
He'll shrink and shrink and shrink and
    shrink,
His skin will be no longer pink,
He'll be so smooth and square and small
He will not know himself at all.
Farewell, Augustus Gloop, farewell!
For soon you'll be a caramel!'

# P is for . . .

## Pemmican

Is it a sticky sweet? Is it a tasty treat? Is it a
strange type of chewy chocolate? No, it is a
pressed cake of meat, fat and berries that
Roald Dahl lived on when he once trekked
across Newfoundland. He also ate boiled
lichen and reindeer moss. Mmmm . . .

## Piker, Miranda Mary

A girl who is allowed to do anything
that she wants – apart from
appear in a Roald Dahl book.
She was cut from the final
version of **Charlie and the
Chocolate Factory**. Snip!

## posh chocs

Roald Dahl loved chocolate bars, but he also used to treat himself to posh chocs from a shop in London.

## Prune, Marvin

A conceited boy – and also a vanishing boy. Marvin Prune appeared in Roald Dahl's earlier draft of **Charlie and the Chocolate Factory**, but never made it to the finished book.

is for...

## Quiz

A. What was the first name of the boy who was sucked up a tube in **Charlie and the Chocolate Factory**?

B. What colour did Violet Beauregarde turn when she chewed the chewing-gum meal?

C. What did Willy Wonka use to make Prince Pondicherry's palace?

D. Whose father poached pheasants?

E. What was the original name for Maltesers?

F. Which drink does the BFG love to guzzle? (Beware: it can give you whizzpops!)

G. Who fed marvellous medicine to his grandma?

26

*H.* What was Matilda's favourite hot drink?

*I.* What type of chocolate is the best chocolate to eat in school?

*J.* Which grandpa went with Charlie to the chocolate factory?

*K.* What was the name of Roald Dahl's favourite Norwegian sweet treat?

*L.* Where do Oompa-Loompas come from?

*M.* What sort of eatable pillows did Willy Wonka make?

*N.* What do Willy Wonka's squirrels take out of their shells?

*O.* In which Norwegian city did the Dahls eat krokaan and ice cream? (Clue: it's the capital of Norway.)

*P.* What did James and his insect friends eat on their trip to New York City?

*Q.* Who ordered fried eggs, bacon, sausages and fried potatoes for the BFG?

*R.* What colour was Roald Dahl's special chocolate box?

*S*. What are Gumtwizzlers and Fizzwinkles and Frothblowers and Spitsizzlers and Gobwangles? (They all appear in **The Giraffe and the Pelly and Me**.)

*T*. The Enormous Crocodile has lots of these. So do dentists. What are they?

*U*. Which green and yellow fruit is a cross between a grapefruit and a tangerine? (Clue: it isn't very pretty.)

*V*. What were Roald Dahl's second most favourite things to eat?

*W*. Who was the most amazing, the most fantastic, the most extraordinary chocolate maker the world has ever seen?

*X*. Which bitter drink was the very first chocolatey thing ever made?

*Y*. Do you like chocolate?

*Z*. Hot chocolate is the perfect bedtime drink. But what sound does it make you do?

**Answers:**

*A*. Augustus. *B*. Blue. *C*. Chocolate. *D*. Danny (the Champion of the World). *E*. Energy Balls. *F*. Frobscottle. *G* George. *H*. Hot chocolate. *I*. Invisible chocolate (invented by Willy Wonka). *J*. Joe. *K*. Krokaan. *L*. Loompaland. *M*. Marshmallow pillows. *N*. Nuts. *O*. Oslo. *P*. Peach! *Q*. The Queen. *R*. Red. *S*. Sweets! *T*. Teeth. *U*. An Ugli fruit. *V*. Vegetables. *W*. Willy Wonka. *X*. Xocoatl. *Y*. Yes. (If you don't, why not?!) *Z*. Zzzz ...

# R is for ...

## Runny chocolate recipe

One of Roald Dahl's favourite chocolate recipes is very easy and tastes whoopsy-good. First, ask an adult to melt a whole

Mars bar in a bowl over boiling water. Then,
pour the runny, chocolatey goo over vanilla
ice cream. Make sure you eat it quickly to
prevent adults gobbling it all!

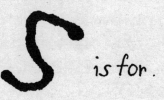

**S** is for...

## Seven glorious years
Roald Dahl believed that the most
gloriumptious chocolate treats were
invented between 1930 and 1937. These
were Aero, Black Magic, Crunchies, Kit Kats,
Maltesers, Mars bars, Quality Street, Rolos
and Smarties.

## Silver ball
When he worked in London, Roald Dahl
rolled a silver ball – about the size of a tennis

ball – from the silver wrappers of his daily chocolate bar.

## Sizzling bacon

Forget the delicious smell of steaming hot chocolate! Roald Dahl thought that the gloriumptious whiff of sizzling bacon was truly the best smell in the whole world.

## Slugburgers

To make these you will need . . . Only joking! But they're on the menu in

**The Magic Finger**.

# Snozzcumber

It's disgustable! It's sickable! It's maggotwise!
It really doesn't taste very nice at all. The
snozzcumber is the BFG's least favourite thing
to eat.

# T is for...

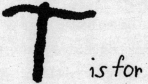

## Teachers

Roald Dahl thought that chocolate was a vital part of everybody's education! He said:

'If I were a headmaster, I would get rid of the history teacher and get a chocolate teacher instead . . . and if I wasn't over-age, I would apply for the job myself.'

# Toothbrush

Chocolate is, unquestionably, a treat of great deliciousness. But dentists aren't so keen, which is why they invented toothbrushes.

# Top chocolate chompers

According to one survey, these are the top ten chocolate-eating countries!

1. Switzerland
2. Austria
3. Ireland
4. Germany

5. Norway

6. Denmark

7. United Kingdom

8. Belgium

9. Sweden

10. USA

## Trout, Herpes

Mike Teavee's original fishy name
in earlier versions of **Charlie
and the Chocolate Factory**!

## Tuck box

At school, Roald Dahl's
tuck box was his most
treasured possession. It
was packed with cake,
biscuits, oranges,
strawberry jam and
– of course – chocolate.

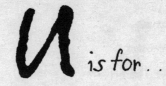

# U is for . . .

## Upside-down monkeys

The Twits only gave their monkeys food and
drink if they balanced upside down.

You'll have to read the book – the right
way up – to find out if the monkeys got
their own back . . .

# V is for . . .

## Vegetables

Roald Dahl's second favourite things to eat (no prizes for guessing his most favourite food!) were vegetables. He thought that broad beans and onions were delumptious.

# W is for...

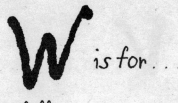

## Waterfall

The only way to mix chocolate properly –
according to Mr Willy Wonka, chocolate-
maker extraordinaire – is to send it gushing
over a waterfall. It churns it up! It pounds and
beats it! It makes it light and frothy!

## Whipple-Scrumpets

Roald Dahl's original name for the Oompa-Loompas.

## Whizzpops

This is what you get if you glug too much frobscottle.

(Oooh, excuse me!)

### Wine gums

These chewy, tangy delights were Roald Dahl's favourite midnight snack.

### Witches' potions

Roald Dahl made scary-looking drinks for his children that he called witches' potions. One drink was made from whizzed-up tinned peaches, milk and green food colouring. It looked revolting, but tasted delicious.

### Wonka's chocolate factory

Mr Willy Wonka's factory wasn't the first. A chocolate factory was built in Bayonne, France, in 1780 – that's 184 years before **Charlie and the Chocolate Factory** was written.

## Wonka's Whipple-Scrumptious Fudgemallow Delight

Charlie Bucket's mouth-watering birthday present. But will there be a Golden Ticket inside ...?

## World Chocolate Awards

The very first World Chocolate Awards took place in January 2005. There were prizes given for twelve delicious chocolate categories, including chocolate bars, filled chocolate, organic chocolate and fair-trade chocolate.

## Wriggling worms

They look so like spaghetti, don't you think?

Well, Mr Twit was fooled.

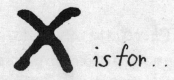 is for...

## xocoatl

This is an Aztec word (pronounced

sho-co-ah-tel) and is a bitter chocolate drink

that came from Mexico. Spanish conqueror
Hernán Cortés took the recipe back to Spain
with him, where it was kept secret for a
hundred years. How mean!

# Y is for...

## Yummy

Chocolate is yummy. It's also delicious,
delumptious and delightful.
And scrumdiddlyumptious.
But don't eat too much
or you'll end up like
Augustus Gloop!

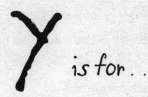

# Z is for...

Zzzz . . .

Roald Dahl once dreamed of being a world-famous chocolate inventor, but then he became an author and invented Willy Wonka instead. Aren't you glad he did?

# TOP SECRET

Here it is . . .
Turn the page to discover 'Spotty Powder' –
a chapter so secret, not only was it
taken out of the original
Charlie and the Chocolate Factory
but, to stop other swizzfigglers sneaking a
peek, you can only read it with the aid
of a mirror!

Read on and enjoy but, whatever you do,
don't let the sneaky Fickelgruber,
Prodnose or Slugworth see it!

'THIS stuff', said Mr Wonka, 'is going to cause chaos in schools all over the world when I get it in the shops.'

The room they now entered had rows and rows of pipes coming straight up out of the floor. The pipes were bent over at the top and they looked like large walking sticks. Out of every pipe there trickled a stream of white crystals. Hundreds of Oompa-Loompas were running to and fro, catching the crystals in little golden boxes and stacking the boxes against the walls.

'Spotty Powder!' exclaimed Mr Wonka, beaming at the company. 'There it is! That's it! Fantastic stuff!'

'It looks like sugar,' said Miranda Piker.

'It's meant to look like sugar,' Mr Wonka said. 'And it tastes like sugar. But it isn't sugar. Oh, dear me, no.'

'Then what is it?' asked Miranda Piker, speaking rather rudely.

'That door over there,' said Mr Wonka, turning away from Miranda and pointing to a small red door at the far end of the room, 'leads directly down to the machine that makes the powder. Twice a day I go down there myself to feed it. But I'm the only one. Nobody ever comes with me.'

They all stared at the little door on which it said **MOST SECRET – KEEP OUT**.

The hum and throb of powerful machinery could be heard coming up from the depths below, and the floor itself was vibrating all the time. The children could feel it through the soles of their shoes.

Miranda Piker now pushed forward and stood in front of Mr Wonka. She was a nasty-looking girl with a smug face and a smirk on her mouth, and whenever she spoke it was always with a voice that seemed to be saying, 'Everybody is a fool except me.'

'OK,' Miranda Piker said, smirking at Mr

Wonka. 'So what's the big news? What's this stuff meant to do when you eat it?'

'Ah-ha', said Mr Wonka, his eyes sparkling with glee. 'You'd never guess that, not in a million years. Now listen. All you have to do is sprinkle it over your cereal at breakfast-time, pretending it's sugar. Then you eat it. And then, exactly five seconds after that, you come out in bright red spots all over your face and neck.'

'What sort of a silly ass wants spots on his face at breakfast-time?' said Miranda Piker.

'Let me finish,' said Mr Wonka. 'So then

your mother looks at you across the table
and says, "My poor child. You must have
chickenpox. You can't possibly go to school
today." So you stay at home. But by lunch-
time, the spots have all disappeared.'

'Terrific!' shouted Charlie. 'That's just what
I want for the day we have exams!'

'That is the ideal time to use it,' said Mr
Wonka. 'But you mustn't do it too often or
it'll give the game away. Keep it for the really
nasty days.'

'Father!' cried Miranda Piker. 'Did you hear
what this stuff does? It's shocking! It mustn't
be allowed!'

Mr Piker, Miranda's father, stepped forward
and faced Mr Wonka. He had a smooth white
face like a boiled onion.

'Now see here, Wonka', he said. 'I happen
to be the headmaster of a large school, and I
won't allow you to sell this rubbish to the
children! It's ... criminal! Why, you'll ruin the

school system of the entire country!'

'I hope so', said Mr Wonka.

'It's got to be stopped!' shouted Mr Piker,
waving his cane.

'Who's going to stop it?' asked Mr Wonka.
'In my factory I make things to please
children. I don't care about grown-ups.'

'I am top of my form', Miranda Piker said,
smirking at Mr Wonka. 'And I've never missed
a day's school in my life.'

'Then it's time you did', Mr Wonka said.

'How dare you!' said Mr Piker.

'All holidays and vacations should be
stopped!' cried Miranda. 'Children are meant

to work, not play.'

'Quite right, my girl', cried Mr Piker, patting
Miranda on the top of the head. 'All work
and no play has made you what you are
today.'

'Isn't she wonderful?' said Mrs Piker,
beaming at her daughter.

'Come on then, Father', cried Miranda.
'Let's go down into the cellar and smash the
machine that makes this dreadful stuff.'

'Forward!' shouted Mr Piker, brandishing his
cane and making a dash for the little red door
on which it said MOST SECRET – KEEP
OUT.

'Stop!' said Mr Wonka. 'Don't go in there!
It's terribly secret!'

'Let's see you stop us, you old goat!'
shouted Miranda.

'We'll smash it to smithereens!' yelled Mr
Piker. And a few seconds later the two of
them had disappeared through the door.

There was a moment's silence. Then, far off
in the distance, from somewhere deep
underground, there came a fearful scream.

'That's my husband!' cried Mrs Piker, going
blue in the face.

There was another scream.

'And that's Miranda!' yelled Mrs Piker,
beginning to hop around in circles. 'What's
happening to them? What have you got
down there, you dreadful beast?'

'Oh, nothing much,' Mr Wonka answered.
'Just a lot of cogs and wheels and chains and
things like that, all going round and round and
round.'

'You villain!' she screamed. 'I know your tricks! You're grinding them into powder! In two minutes my darling Miranda will come pouring out of one of those dreadful pipes, and so will my husband!'

'Of course', said Mr Wonka. 'That's part of the recipe.'

'It's what!'

'We've got to use one or two schoolmasters occasionally or it wouldn't work.'

'Did you hear him?' shrieked Mrs Piker, turning to the others. 'He admits it! He's nothing but a cold-blooded murderer!'

Mr Wonka smiled and patted Mrs Piker gently on the arm. 'Dear lady,' he said, 'I was only joking.'

'Then why did they scream?' snapped Mrs Piker. 'I distinctly heard them scream!'

'Those weren't screams,' Mr Wonka said. 'They were laughs.'

'My husband never laughs,' said Mrs Piker.
Mr Wonka flicked his fingers, and up came
an Oompa-Loompa.

'Kindly escort Mrs Piker to the boiler
room,' Mr Wonka said. 'Don't fret, dear lady,'
he went on, shaking Mrs Piker warmly by the
hand. 'They'll all come out in the wash.
There's nothing to worry about. Off you go.
Thank you for coming. Farewell! Goodbye! A
pleasure to meet you!'

'Listen, Charlie!' said Grandpa Joe. 'The
Oompa-Loompas are starting to sing again!'

'Oh, Miranda Mary Piker!' sang the five
Oompa-Loompas dancing about and laughing
and beating madly on their tiny drums.

'Oh, Miranda Mary Piker,
How could anybody like her,
Such a priggish and revolting little kid.
So we said, "Why don't we fix her
In the Spotty-Powder mixer

Then we're bound to like her better
than we did."
Soon this child who is so vicious
Will have gotten quite delicious,
And her classmates will have surely
understood
That instead of saying, "Miranda!
Oh, the beast! We cannot stand her!",
They'll be saying, "Oh, how useful
and how good!"'

# THE ROALD DAHL MUSEUM AND STORY CENTRE

'Tremendous Things Are in Store for You!'

Are you one of Roald Dahl's biggest fans? If you are, then we have got some splendiferous news for you!

As you probably know, Roald Dahl lived in Great Missenden, a quiet village in Buckinghamshire where he wrote all of his stories for kids. But did you know that in spring 2005, Great Missenden will become the most scrumdiddlyumptious place in the world when the Roald Dahl Museum and Story Centre opens its doors for the first time?

The Museum and Story Centre will tell the eventful tale of Roald Dahl's life, using photographs and film. Interactive displays will help you to discover more about his Norwegian family, his schooldays, his time as a World War Two pilot and how he became a world-famous writer. It will also be jam-packed with stuff about how to write, a replica of Roald's writing hut and facts about other brilliant authors. There will even be a chance to make up stories of your own!

# THE ROALD DAHL FOUNDATION

## Doing **wonkalicious** things

Providing practical support for children with
brain, blood and literacy problems

**What is the Roald Dahl Foundation?**
As well as being a great storyteller, Roald Dahl was
also a man who gave generously of his time and
money to help people in need, especially children.
After he died in 1990, his widow, Felicity, set up
the Roald Dahl Foundation to continue this
generous tradition. Our support spreads far and
wide. Since we began, the Foundation has given
over £4 million across the UK.

The Foundation aims to help children and young
people in practical ways and in three areas that
were particularly important to Roald Dahl during
his lifetime: neurology, haematology
and literacy. We make grants to
hospitals and charities, as well
as to individual children and
their families.

## Supporting the
## Roald Dahl Foundation

Funded partly through the Foundation's original endowment, we also benefit from a range of fundraising, most notably the national sponsored reading event Readathon®. In addition, we are proud of the Friends of Roald Dahl Foundation who arrange a programme of local events, the many schoolchildren who fundraise on our behalf and our Payroll Giving supporters. Finally, we are able to benefit from an ambitious programme of new orchestral music for children based on Roald Dahl's stories and rhymes, specially commissioned on our behalf.

To find out more about the Roald Dahl Foundation or to make an online donation, visit our website at www.roalddahlfoundation.org.

The Roald Dahl Foundation is a
registered charity no.1004230

# D is for **DAHL**

A is for Adenoids

B is for Blabbermouth

C is for Chocolate...

**T**his is NOT a biography! This an A–Z of amazing facts – some funny, some silly, all true – that brings to life the world's favourite children's writer. A real treasure trove to dip into, or read from cover to cover – it's the next best thing to meeting the man himself!

# Charlie and the Chocolate Factory

wriggle-sweets

hair toffee

luminous lollies

rainbow drops

Mr Wonka's inventions are out of this world. He's thought up every kind of sweet imaginable in his amazing chocolate factory, but no one has ever seen inside, or met Mr Wonka! Charlie Bucket can't believe his luck when he finds a Golden Ticket and wins the trip of a lifetime around the famous chocolate factory. He could never have *dreamed* what surprises lie in store!

# The Giraffe and the Pelly and Me

**What does a window-cleaning company need?**

A bucket, a ladder and a cleaner? How about a pelican, a giraffe and a monkey? Not the usual ingredients, but this is a window-cleaning company with a difference. Join Billy as he makes friends with three amazing animals and gets up to some thrilling adventures.